The Urbana Free Library

To renew: call **217-367-4057**
or go to **urbanafreelibrary.org**
and select **My Account**

SCARED

BY SAVINA COLLINS

ILLUSTRATED BY
ANITA DUFALLA

ROurke
Educational Media
rourkeeducationalmedia.com

Before & After Reading Activities

Teaching Focus:
Concepts of Print: Ending Punctuation- Have students locate the ending punctuation for sentences in the book. Count how many times a period, question mark, or exclamation point is used. Which one is used the most? What is the purpose for each ending punctuation mark? Practice reading these sentences with appropriate expression.

Before Reading:

Building Academic Vocabulary and Background Knowledge

Before reading a book, it is important to set the stage for your child or student by using pre-reading strategies. This will help them develop their vocabulary, increase their reading comprehension, and make connections across the curriculum.

1. Read the title and look at the cover. *Let's make predictions about what this book will be about.*
2. Take a picture walk by talking about the pictures/photographs in the book. Implant the vocabulary as you take the picture walk. Be sure to talk about the text features such as headings, the Table of Contents, glossary, bolded words, captions, charts/diagrams, or index.
3. Have students read the first page of text with you then have students read the remaining text.
4. Strategy Talk – use to assist students while reading.
    - Get your mouth ready
    - Look at the picture
    - Think…does it make sense
    - Think…does it look right
    - Think…does it sound right
    - Chunk it – by looking for a part you know
5. Read it again.

Content Area Vocabulary
Use glossary words in a sentence.

goose bumps
lightning
thunderstorm
trickle

After Reading:

Comprehension and Extension Activity

After reading the book, work on the following questions with your child or students in order to check their level of reading comprehension and content mastery.

1. *What does Deon think of thunderstorms? (Summarize)*
2. *What does Deon do when he is scared? (Asking Questions)*
3. *What makes you scared? (Text to self connection)*
4. *What can you do next time you feel scared? (Asking Questions)*

Extension Activity

Make a brave puppet. Use a lunch bag, crayons, yarn, and glue to make a puppet of yourself being brave. This will be your brave puppet to help you when you feel scared.

TABLE OF CONTENTS

THE STORM

Deon looks out the window.

The sky is dark and cloudy.

Lightning flashes.

Thunder booms.

FEELING SCARED

The **thunderstorm** is loud.

It makes Deon feel scared.

Deon has **goose bumps.**

11

Tears **trickle** down his cheeks.

Boom!

Deon runs to his room.

He squeezes his eyes shut.

16

He covers his ears.

17

He takes a big breath.

He sings a song.

19

SUNSHINE

After the storm, Deon goes outside.

The storm watered the flowers!

Storms aren't so bad, Deon thinks.

PICTURE GLOSSARY

goose bumps (goos buhmps): When you are cold or frightened tiny bumps appear on your skin.

lightning (LITE-ning): A flash of light in the sky when electricity moves between clouds, or between clouds and the ground.

thunderstorm (THUHN-dur-storm): A storm with heavy rain, thunder, and lightning.

trickle (TRIK-uhl): Flowing very slowly in a thin stream, or falling in drops.

ABOUT THE AUTHOR

Savina Collins lives in Florida with her husband and 5 adventurous kids. She loves watching her kids surf at the beach. When she is not at the beach, Savina enjoys reading and taking long walks.

Meet The Author!
www.meetREMauthors.com

Library of Congress PCN Data

Scared/ Savina Collins
(I Have Feelings!)
ISBN 978-1-68342-140-5 (hard cover)
ISBN 978-1-68342-182-5 (soft cover)
ISBN 978-1-68342-213-6 (e-Book)
Library of Congress Control Number: 2016956532

Rourke Educational Media
Printed in the United States of America, North Mankato, Minnesota

www.rourkeeducationalmedia.com

Edited by: Keli Sipperley
Cover design and interior design by: Rhea Magaro-Wallace

Also Available as:

ROURKE'S
e-Books